#2 dive into danger

ANIMAL RESCUES

#2 dive into danger

KELLY MILNER HALLS

darbycreek
MINNEAPOLIS

Darby Creek
A division of Lerner Publishing Group, Inc.
241 First Avenue North
Minneapolis, MN 55401 USA

For reading levels and more information, look up this title at
www.lernerbooks.com.

Additional images: © iStockphoto.com/benz190 (grunge texture); © iStockphoto.com/
Piotr Krześlak (paper texture).

Main body text set in Janson Text LT Std 12/17.5.
Typeface provided by Adobe Systems.

Library of Congress Cataloging-in-Publication Data

Halls, Kelly Milner, 1957– author.
    Dive into danger / Kelly Milner Halls ; illustrated by Phil Parks.
        pages cm. — (Animal rescues ; #2)
    Summary: Fourteen-year-old Pudge spends most of his time in the basement
avoiding his marine biologist father and playing World of Warcraft, but when
missing school earns him a suspension and he joins his father at work, he must
summon real courage to help a mother humpback whale.
    ISBN 978-1-4677-7220-4 (lb : alk. paper) — ISBN 978-1-4677-9565-4
(pb : alk. paper) — ISBN 978-1-4677-9566-1 (eb pdf)
        [1. Fathers and sons—Fiction. 2. Overweight persons—Fiction. 3. Fantasy
games—Fiction. 4. Humpback whale—Fiction. 5. Whales—Fiction. 6. Animal
rescue—Fiction.] I. Parks, Phil, illustrator. II. Title.
PZ7.1.H33Div 2016
[Fic]—dc23   2015017910

Manufactured in the United States of America
1 – BP – 12/31/15

To my daughter Vanessa, who kept my *World of Warcraft* references on the mark and spurred me on, come rain or shine

CHAPTER ONE
Once a Pudge, Always a Pudge

Sunday

In my dreams, I swim like an orca. Sleek. Powerful. Fearless. Then I wake up.

It's not that I can't swim. I do okay in a pool. But toss me into the Pacific Ocean and I panic. There's no way to tell what's swimming next to you. A dolphin and a shark look alike until it's too late to escape. Most people get that, but my dad? Not so much.

"There's a world beyond that basement,"

he says again and again. And he's a biologist for the Marine Mammal Center in Sausalito, California. He could literally write a book about the world beyond my world. "You could be so much more than you are," he says. But all I can hear is, "You're not good enough." And all I can think is, "He's right."

It's not his fault. He was born to be a tan, aquatic giant with both brawn and brain. I was born to be Pudge. That's what he calls me. It started as my mom's nickname for a fat little toddler, and it stuck—even after she left us. I doubt Dad even remembers my name is Austin.

Most days, I push past his disappointment. He lives upstairs. I live in the basement. He leaves for work at six a.m. I wake up at seven for school. We only chat at dinner—small talk.

"How was your day?"

"Did we get any mail?"

If my weight comes up, the peace is shattered, so it doesn't come up. Silence takes its place.

"Better hit the books," he says when things get awkward. So I head down for the night. He thinks homework is hard for me, but it's not. I may be fat, but I'm not stupid. Forty minutes and all the assignments I didn't finish at school are done. Then I'm free to play World of Warcraft, my favorite video game—as long as he doesn't know about it.

"Video games are a waste of energy," he says, "illusions to distract you from real life." He said the same thing about my art and my mother's dream of being a singer. I respectfully disagree. Drawing keeps me focused. Every doodle helps me learn. And RPGs—role-playing games—*are* my life. When I play WoW, I'm the guy he wants me to be.

I haven't been playing WoW long, but when I sign on to the game from my laptop, I am transformed. I am Hippocrates, an undead zombie priest and healer, reanimated by the power of a banshee queen. And while I'm a beginner now, I have a goal. I want to level up and earn a spot in one of the most prestigious guilds in the game—the Dead Druid Society. I am committed.

I check my friend list and see my best friend Duffy is already logged in. His handsome blood elf character Cyrano is bounding across a tropical landscape, flirting with any player he thinks is a girl.

As I watch, a conversation bubble appears on the colorful play screen.

"Cyrano greets Briarrose."

Briarrose runs from my friend. "Your loss," he types.

Another bubble opens.

"Cyrano greets Silverstar."

Silverstar waves and then mounts her skeletal horse to gallop away.

"Not getting much play," I type in a private message. "Did you brush those elfin teeth before you hit the game, or are you rocking corn chips?"

Duffy types LOL and then Skypes me so we can talk. "I gargled with vodka," he says. "Does that count, Pudge?"

Duffy is only fourteen. He doesn't drink and neither do I. There's no way he's gargled with alcohol. But I let the fiction slide because I get why he said it. In an RPG, you can pretend to be someone you're not without getting hurt, like trying on a pair of Jordans you could never afford.

"Ready to rumble?" he asks, and I say yes. If we want to level up, we'll have to master this five-person dungeon and a stack of quests and other missions. But Duffy loves to do battle. I'll fight enemies too, but I'm not the warrior he is. In fact, I'm hoping to search for herbs after the fight. I'll need ingredients to make powerful healing potions.

A troll warlock waits with us. She swings her staff. Her faithful pet leaps and sways, anxious for the battle to begin. Weird how pushing a few buttons can make you feel pumped. But no one can play until two more important players join the group.

When two other players finally join us, the healer and the tank come together—probably friends like Duffy and me. Duff lets out a little whistle. "Check out the pandaren tank," he says. "She's decked out in heirlooms. We're in good hands."

"Heirlooms?" I ask, turning to inspect the little panda's gear.

"Expensive hand-me-downs from a more experienced character," he says. "Pompomz may look new like us, but the person playing her has chops. Let's do this!"

Without hesitation, the tank enters first to draw the enemy fire. The sheer chaos would slaughter a lesser player, but Pompomz is fearless. She shines with confidence, so I settle back to watch her work.

A conversation bubble appears. "Keep a safe distance and watch out for acid," she warns Duffy.

"It's not my first rodeo," he types and then runs past her yelling, "Die, you scumbags!" No one is surprised when he slips in a puddle of the fluorescent ooze she warned him about.

"Welcome to the rodeo," she types, and I can't help laughing.

"LOL," I type. "My friend got slimed and schooled."

Duffy complains, but I don't care. Because Pompomz is smiling.

Then I notice—his health bar is shrinking, so his battle and this life is about to be over. I worry and wish I had the confidence to heal him myself. But the real healer is watching too. Just as Duffy starts to fade, he gracefully raises his healing elfin arms and a pulsing stream of green light bursts from his fingertips. Duffy is enveloped, and in an instant, his health is restored.

Renewed, his war cries sound more dangerous than ever. But there's nothing truly ferocious about Duffy or any of us.

People think gaming causes real-life violence, but it's not true. Video games keep our inner beasts in check—the same way green plastic army men did when we were little. When we tossed those little guys off the roof, we weren't learning how to kill people. We were learning to think. It's the same with RPGs.

"You nearly bought the farm, Duff," I say.

"You know it, Pudge," he answers, "but that hot little tank was unstoppable. And did you see that healer? Holy jeez, he was amazing."

"Yeah," I whisper. "He really was. And I want to be just like him."

"You will be," Duff says without a trace of sarcasm. "It's your destiny."

I feel a lump in my throat. Yeah, I kind of love that guy.

That night I dream of my destiny the minute my head hits the pillow. And a pandaren girl named Pompom is standing right beside me.

CHAPTER TWO
Back to School

Monday

A note dangles from the refrigerator door when I wake up Monday morning.

"Don't forget your research project," Dad has written. *Forget* is underlined three times. He's not wrong. I get distracted when a task doesn't interest me. And research is dull. It would be different if they let me write about what I love. But who cares about a war that started in 1914?

"Got it," I scribble on the note. I shove a sandwich and a bag of chips in my backpack and head to class—on time.

"Austin," Miss Grayson says as I take the desk next to Duffy. She is young for a middle school teacher and way too cheerful for a predawn history class. But she's the only person who uses my real name. And I can't lie. I like it—a lot. "Can I assume you've settled on a topic for your WWI research project? It's deadline day."

"I was thinking of art," I say. It's a bluff. I have no idea what I actually mean.

"Perfect," she says softly. My mouth falls open in surprise. "I dig the sketches on your notebook. Now take it to the next level."

The volume of her voice explodes as she turns to the class, "Austin will investigate the art of wartime propaganda, one of my favorite subjects. I'll lend him a book to get started."

Duffy shakes his head, calling my bluff. "No one should be that lucky," he whispers.

But when he admits he still doesn't have a topic, she assigns him Manfred von Richthofen—the Red Baron. So there is plenty of luck to go around. She hands him the baron's autobiography, declaring the baron the father of aerial combat. Duff holds the book like a holy relic.

"And for the mighty Austin," she says, "*World War I Posters*—238 pages of truths or lies, artfully told." It's a huge, hardcover book full of iconic images, including Uncle Sam pointing at me, and it's a thing of beauty. I don't hear a word anyone says the rest of the period. I'm hypnotized by art deco masterpieces on the pages.

"Remember," Miss Grayson announces. "Study your topic and study it well. Compile a bibliography to prove it. No short cuts, no cheat codes. But once the study ends, let the creativity begin. Do something brilliant to reveal what you've learned. But what *brilliant* means is up to you."

For the first time in my life, research might be worthwhile. I text my father. "Doing research at the Marino Public Library after school. Eat without me." I don't tell him how excited I am because he'd never believe me. But Duffy's up for the library too, so we walk over after the last bell rings.

In less than three hours, my spiral notebook is full of names and dates and catchphrases. Duffy is asleep across the table. When I'm ready to go, I kick his foot.

"What?" he screams, drool dripping from the corners of his mouth. The aging night librarian shoots a death stare his way. "Relax," he tells her, shrugging his shoulders, which irritates her more. But she goes back to what she was doing before his outburst, convinced the noise won't continue.

"The ladies love you," I whisper sarcastically. "Especially the old ones."

"Cougars," he answers, with a wink. Ew, I think. Then it gets worse. "That little tank was into me too . . . last night," he says.

"Pompomz?" I ask. "No way."

"Way," he says. "Wait. You know her name?"

"You don't?" I challenge him. His face goes blank, so I win the point. Then I smile, wondering if she might be online.

"Howdy, Pudge." I hear Dad's voice from the kitchen as I open the front door.

He's not in bed, and he's in a good mood. Seems the humpback whales have been spotted near the islands of Farallon National Wildlife Refuge in the San Francisco Bay. Charting their migration is his favorite duty. So I decide to hang out with him for a while. We raid the Lucky Charms as we talk.

"So you went to the library," he says, wrangling colorful marshmallows onto his spoon. "Does that mean you picked your research topic?"

"It does," I say. "I'm researching propaganda art during World War I."

Dad smiles. It's not his "I'll have to tolerate this," smile but a real one—from the heart. I feel my cheeks burn, but I'm not sure why.

"Great topic," he says. "Did you come up with it yourself?"

The answer represents a gray area, but I'm not ready to let go of his approval. So I wander near deception. "I did," I say. "But Miss Grayson approved it, so I've already started."

"Fantastic," he says. "Can't wait to see what you do with it, Austin."

We nod, smiling as we finish the cereal. He's glad I found a decent topic. I'm glad he remembers my name. I might have told him so, if I wasn't so afraid of letting him down. Instead, I say, "Yeah, guess I better sleep on it. Good night, Dad."

I head for the basement in full-on retreat. Besides, the game awaits.

Monday Night

Wandering the game's Hillsbrad Foothills as
a rotting corpse can be dangerous—especially
without Duffy there to defend me. But he's not
online and I am determined to collect herbs.
Mageroyal and bruiseweed are ripe for the
picking here, not to mention other quests for
extra experience points. So I press on.

I collect a few quests from the computer-
generated characters in the town of Tarren

Mill—mostly undead types like me. "Kill six night wolves and bring me their pelts," a quest giver says. "I will give you a potion in return."

I accept but immediately regret it. Killing video game animals is easy, but it feels wrong. They're minding their own business, full of light and color, and then you trap them with a burst of energy. They fall like flies in winter, and it gets me every time.

Bugsy farts under my computer desk and lightens the mood. "Good one," I say rubbing my sock foot against his backside. Poor guy lost an eye before we got him. Someone thought it was fun to throw rocks at a baby pit bull—someone with good aim. He still flinches if I toss him even a dog biscuit, so I'm extra gentle. Wish I could do the same with computer-generated wolves.

"Sorry," I whisper as I kill the last one and collect my potion. Now it's time for the herbs.

Hiding from the region's cyber wildlife isn't too hard. Forest creepers aren't deadly unless you make the giant spiders mad. And the gray bears hardly notice I'm hiding behind giant spruce trees. As long as I don't slide down the face of a cliff, I've got this.

"Come to Papa," I think as I bend down to pluck my third batch of pink mageroyal flowers. They slip easily into my bag, and I feel content. Then I see it, the thorny vines of bruiseweed—about ten yards ahead of me. I am so excited, I fail to notice the Black War Gryphon touch down behind me. Erasto, its high-level rider, dismounts and I freeze.

The gnome rogue waves at me.

I hesitate. The gnome is half Hippocrates's height, but his level dwarfs my zombie healer. Even his elaborate matching black and red armor is a testament to how long he's been playing. I can only imagine the time that went into such an acquisition.

Eventually, I have Hippocrates wave back. The gnome fights for the Alliance, and I ally with the Horde. Speech between such ancient enemies is impossible, so only a few preprogrammed actions allow us to communicate. I could attack him, but it would be meaningless. Even my strongest curse wouldn't faze him. But conversation isn't necessary when the rogue disappears from sight. After all, stealth is a rogue's bread and butter.

I stand motionless for a time, but he doesn't reappear. So I collect the bruiseweed I spotted. Maybe Erasto was just passing through, I think. No reason for him to linger. There's nothing for his powerful, high-level character to gain here. I think the encounter is over, until the attack begins.

Hippocrates suddenly stops dead in his tracks, but I'm no longer controlling his motions. He begins to sway and wobble like a wounded cartoon character. Even colorful stars dance around his head. We've been stunned.

"What?" I say aloud. Then Erasto reappears, chuckling at my discomfort before vanishing like before. I heave a sigh and start to shake the thumping off, only to be stunned again. Dang! He's playing with me, like an orca plays with a seal. I'm plenty creeped out, but I'm also really annoyed. Doesn't this guy have anything better to do? Without purpose or cause, he wants my character dead.

I try to run, but my zombie priest is no match for the rogue's obvious skills. As my character falls to the ground, as my light begins to fade, I pound one last word on my keyboard, a word that won't even appear on the game screen: *"Why?"* And I realize, it wouldn't matter if it did. The rogue is determined to end Hippocrates's life. I am amazed at the senseless brutality of it all. But what happens next amazes me more.

Like an angel of mercy, a high-level pandaren hunter with a glimmering gold cloud serpent suddenly descends. With a whistle, she calls her pet, an enormous mastiff dog named Digby, and together they strike Erasto with unyielding ferocity. Arrows fly from her bow, and the canine's jaws clamp like a vise. The rogue must be as stunned and confused as I was, but he has no time to type or question. And I think she would ignore him, even if he did.

No match for the powerful hunter, Erasto tries to run, but it's too late. She launches a trap from her bow, which wraps around the rogue's feet. Then a burst of flame overwhelms him, and he is dead—until he regenerates again at the nearest graveyard. As my health is slowly restored, his body evaporates, just a few feet from where he tried to kill me. The fight is over, and the pandaren girl is victorious.

"Hello," she types, requesting a private message conversation. "Are you okay?"

I am grateful to say, "I'm fine, thanks to your mad skills. No thanks to my own." She types LOL.

"It's not my first rodeo," she types. And for the first time since the fates shifted, I take time to look at her name—Pompom, a high-level character, a member of my dream guild, the

Dead Druid Society. Now I know who passed top-level armor down to a low-level dungeon tank called Pompomz.

"So nice to meet you, Pompom," I type.

"Don't you mean, we meet again?" she types. I picture her smiling. "Just call me Pompom, with or without the z."

My rescuer revealed, I am more than a little psyched. What if that tough little tank wasn't into Duffy after all? What if she was into me? Yeah, now she's not the only one smiling.

"Thanks for knocking him out," I say. "What did he have against me?"

"You're low level," she says, "a newb. That's enough for some dirtbag gamers."

"But you're okay with newbs?" I ask. I'm glad she can't see me face-plant my blushing cheeks into the palms of my hands.

"I'm okay with smart newbs," she says. "But more than that, I really hate bullies."

I rub Bugsy's belly with my foot. "Yeah," I type. "We have that in common."

"Tell me about it next time," she says. "My homework is calling."

"Another day, another story," I type. "Good night, Pompom."

"Sounds like a plan," she types. "Good night, Hippo."

I smile and say it aloud—"Hippo." For the first time in my life, I don't mind being compared to a large, barrel-shaped animal. Coming from Pompom, it feels pretty nice.

CHAPTER FOUR
Library Multitasking

Tuesday

"Good morning, eighth graders," Miss Grayson beams as we stumble into class. "Raise your hand if you'd like to discuss your research goals." Not a hand shoots up, but Miss Grayson is unfazed.

"Duffy, what's your plan to celebrate the Red Baron? Suggestion: The word 'Snoopy' better not cross your lips." Duffy's head crashes against his desk, but he's only kidding.

Dude doesn't know the meaning of retreat. He pops up again to claim Miss Grayson's approval.

"I'm going to the aviation museum this weekend," he says. "My father is a photographer for the *San Francisco Chronicle*, so we're going to do a photo essay on the biplanes of World War I. Sound good?"

"Excellent," she says. "But go easy on the 'we.' This is not your father's assignment." Duffy salutes as Miss Grayson searches for another volunteer. Her eyes shift just a few inches.

"Austin," she says. "What did you think of the book I lent you? Are you feeling the fine art of propaganda, my visionary? The wonder of the media blitz?"

I didn't have to pretend. Every poster in the book was amazing, not just the artwork but the way the words inspired sympathy or patriotism or rebellion. "Don't read American History, Make It!" "Our Boys Need Sox! Knit Your

Bit!" I couldn't wait to know more about them, and I admitted it.

"Only one thing to do then," she says. "Head for the public library."

"Now?" I say.

"Duffy, you keep him out of trouble. Be back in time for lunch. I'll give you a pass and let your second-period teacher, Mr. Johnson, know. Who wants library duty tomorrow?"

Dozens of hands shoot up, and I am amazed. Good teachers are like stealth bombers. You're just sitting there, and they drop information into your brain. Boom! Suddenly, you're hooked. You've got to have more. The library can totally hook you up—especially a public library without Internet filters.

It's raining as we walk down the block to the Marino Public Library. But our moods are shining like 14 karat gold. Two hours off campus without getting in trouble? Duff and I call that priceless.

I push the door open wide and Duff follows me in. "Check it out," I say. "They've got a tournament."

"A tournament of what?" he says.

Duff hasn't seen the notice on the bulletin board, but I have. The library is hosting a World of Warcraft tournament. "May the best in Azeroth win," the poster says. We've been leveling up, but I'm pretty sure Hippocrates still doesn't stand a chance to win. Still, playing could be fun.

"Check it out," I say, and Duffy's eyes widen.

"Dude," he says. "Where do I sign up?"

"Right here!" A librarian chimes in. She's half the age of the night librarian from yesterday. She brushes violet hair out of her eyes and slides a clipboard into Duffy's hands. Her silver nail polish reflects the library light as she hands a second clipboard to me. "We need Horde and Alliance, any level. You can win gift cards to GameStop and Barnes & Noble, and there will be pizza.

Did I mention admission is free?"

"I'm in," I say, programming the details—Friday at five o'clock—into my cell phone.

"Hey, Silver Tips," Duffy says, and the librarian smiles. "Do you have the bandwidth for a decent WoW tournament? Library Internet is usually a little slow."

"Was," the young librarian says with a grin. "Think upgrades. Type in the library password, and you're good to go. And you can call me Miss S."

"Sick!" Duffy says, and I can tell something more is on his mind.

"It's great," I say. "But if I don't get some research done, I'll be working on my project, not playing the game."

So while Duffy learns more about the servers and computer upgrades, I crack more books about World War I, hoping for more than the most obvious facts. I need inspiration. My father is watching this time, so I'd really like to do things right.

When I've scanned every book I can find, I turn to the Internet. Duff sees the spark of inspiration before I do, and it's a doozy. We've found another WWI propaganda poster, this one sporting the face of a white-haired pit bull wearing a deep blue Navy cap. "The American Watch Dog," the poster proclaims. "We're not looking for trouble, but we're ready for it."

"Now you're looking at Bugsy pictures?" Duffy says. "How are you going to sell that to Miss Grayson?" Bam! Inspiration strikes with a vengeance, and suddenly my project comes into focus.

"Can you come over tonight?" I asked him. "We'll need your camera, a couple of hats, and my one-eyed dog."

Duffy shows up at six—the same time our meat lover's pizza is delivered. The guy has junk food radar. We head for the basement to eat and work. By the time I start my third slice of pizza, Duffy has finished his sixth. He should be twice my size, but he isn't. Nature loves a joke, I guess.

We've saved some of the meat for Bugsy. Call it dog model incentives. I position a bright red velvet cloth in the corner of my basement to cover the seventies-era shag carpeting. Next, I set up a super-sized, white trifold poster board as a backdrop around the velvet. Add one beefy bribe, and our model takes his place—right in the middle of the velvet where I want him.

"Good boy," I say as he licks my fingers for the last greasy drop. He's such a good-natured dog. It's hard to believe people force pit bulls to fight one another. I get it, their jaws are really strong. I'll never win a game of tug-of-war with Bugsy. He'd hang on for days, if I made him. And that's the other thing. They are incredibly obedient and loyal. Bugs would do almost anything I told him to, just to please me.

That's part of why people fight pit bulls. Because they're so eager to please, they'll keep fighting to the death. Breaks my heart.

Owners of fight dogs pretend the animals love it, but they don't. No animal fights to the death in nature without a really good reason—defending its pack or its puppies. They'll fight for food, but not to the death. Eventually, one side wins and the other runs away.

Pit bulls fight to please their owners, and it's wrong. So I want to do something about it.

"I brought hats," Duffy says, "and little clothes." His little sister has dolls so the selection is pretty good. He sets a pint-sized purple cowboy hat on Bugsy's head, and it's adorable.

"Awww . . . " we both say at the exact same moment, and then we laugh. He punches me in the shoulder and I call him a punk, just to prove we're still pretty manly.

"What's our end game?" Duffy says, as he hands me his digital Canon SLR camera.

"Propaganda," I say. "If opinion posters helped change the course of World War I, maybe they can help stop dog fighting too."

"Study the past to change the future?" Duffy says. I nod. "Miss Grayson is going to kiss you on the mouth."

"I'd settle for a B+," I say as I try another hat on Bugsy.

CHAPTER FIVE
Win, Lose, or Draw

Tuesday Night

Duffy heads home after we upload the pictures to my computer—150 shots of Bugsy in fashion attire. A couple are hilarious: picture a one-eyed, wet-nosed bride. But most of them are pretty dumb—nothing I'd share with Miss Grayson. I'm not sure what to do, so I take a break. I go online.

Duffy's blood elf checks in soon after.

"Need a Bugsy break?" he Skypes.

"Let's do a dungeon," I say. Beating up imaginary bad guys might clear my mind. Our levels have risen enough to qualify for a fresh set of dungeons. That means tougher challenges, it's true. But it also means beefed-up loot, so we're in. Almost immediately, the other three players we need arrive—a mage for damage, a death knight tank, and a shaman healer complete our group. We begin on a cliff face, a massive bridge decorated with spikes that leads us into a thick mist.

"Ominous," Duffy says with approval. He's enjoying this. I'm not so sure.

The tank does what he's built to do. He draws fire and takes damage so we won't have to. Bit by bit, patrols of computer-generated orcs with ferocious hunting hounds fall before him, and soon we are ready to tackle Watchkeeper, the dungeon's first boss and all-around bad guy.

He's a nasty one, enormous with nightmarish red and gold armor. Confidently the death knight tank baits him, pulling him closer and closer. The enemies suddenly charge us without reserve. It should be an even fight, but something is wrong. The tank's health is draining, but nobody is replenishing it. My stomach drops as I realize our shaman has vanished. Our healer is gone.

"Heal him," Duffy yells.

"Me?" I say. "I can't, can I?" Horrified, I watch as our tank falls to the floor with a scream. But Watchkeeper's bloodlust is not so easily quieted. His hungry red eyes turn to Duffy next, and he freezes in fear.

"Okay then," Duffy yelps, "heal me!"

A curse word slips out of my mouth.

"Exactly," Duffy says. "So engage, dude! Do whatever you have to do to save us."

I know he's right. I may not be ready, in my mind, but there is no time left to wonder. I raise my bony arms, say a little prayer, and wait for the magic to begin. My spells and potions have been gathering dust; it's time to try them out.

Flash after flash of white light shoots from my Hippocratic hands, and Duffy shines like an angel in plate armor. I can hear him cackling with delight. He isn't geared to tank for us. He's built to hit and hit hard, not to take this kind of punishment. Even so, his massive two-handed sword glints with each strike, without so much as a shield to protect him. Somehow, my spells replenish his health each time it dips dangerously low.

"You're kicking butt," Duffy whoops. "And so am I!"

Soon Watchkeeper's bodyguards begin to fall. The mage's spells and Duffy's sword do the heavy lifting while I do the healing. Watchkeeper roars with rage as his minions fall. He finally collapses in a heap on the dungeon floor, and Duffy roars, strong and victorious.

"I'm the tank," he laughs, "and you're my healer! Didn't I tell you?"

Watchkeeper has hardly fallen before

Duffy's elf breaks out in dance. My spell-building mana is all but spent, and there is nothing more to drink. But—somehow—we've survived. Stunned, I gaze at the screen.

"Nice," the mage types. He has some colorful words of his own to describe the shaman healer that bailed on us, but I can't be mad. With the enemies vanquished, I let myself laugh a little too.

"Told you so," Duffy chuckles again. "You have a resurrection spell, don't you? Not that tanking hasn't been a blast, but you should probably heal our poor death knight too. He's over there."

"Right," I say, turning to the death knight's character corpse. Within a few seconds, a beacon of golden light surrounds him. He pops back up like a cartoon, still brooding in black armor. I have to say, tanking looked better on Duffy.

The death knight tank doesn't even say thank you. He just queues up to find a replacement healer to add a fifth to our now four-man crew. It's Duffy's turn to sling colorful words. I laugh at his dramatic defense of my wobbly healing, but I can't be upset. I've just ridden an awesome roller coaster. Duffy said healing was my destiny, and I'm starting to believe he was right.

By morning, all doubt is erased after Hippocrates comes to me in a dream. The photos of Bugsy float like ghosts around his zombie head. His gaze moves from image to image to image. Then, one by one, they disappear into his brain, as I watch. He speaks, as a pencil-thin beam of light flows like a laser from his fingertips.

"Doubt and limits lift," he says, "when you truly see your challenge. All things are possible as pictures move from the mind to the hand to the page."

"That's it!" I shout, as I wake in a start. "I won't turn in a photo. I'll turn in original art."

Now that's what I call magic.

CHAPTER SIX
Suspended Animation

Wednesday

An 11 × 17 art pad protrudes from my backpack the next morning when I head for school. It rests safely against a laptop full of pit bull pictures—a laptop I'm probably not supposed to take out of the house. But I want to start drawing while the dream is still fresh in my mind, and my reference pictures are saved on the drive.

"That's genius," Duffy says when I explain my project's new direction. "But where are you going to draw? You won't even let me watch you, much less a bunch of idiots at school."

"Good point," I say. "But I thought maybe we could go back to the library to work. Miss Grayson might give us a pass."

"I don't know, Pudge," Duffy says. "We just went Monday and a lot of other kids have work to do." He has a point, but I ask Miss Grayson just the same. The arch of her eyebrow says no, but then she surprises me.

"One hour," she says. "Stay a minute longer than first period and you turn into a pumpkin. I will tell Mr. Johnson to expect you in class."

"I promise," I say, and Duffy agrees. So we head back to the MPL.

I pick a table at the back of the library, as far from the computer bank as I can get. Duffy grabs the first PC he sees. That's not a bad thing. Duffy can be a real distraction. I pull out my laptop and supplies and get to work. Filtering through the Bugsy pictures,

I see dog smile after dog smile because he's such a happy dude. Then I see it. The shot that sets him apart.

He's wearing a dress-up tiara and necklace, so it should be silly, but it's not. He's gazing off in the distance—probably listening to a dog bark outside. But his eye looks wistful. And you can see where his other eye once was, the fur-covered shadow of what used to be. Just looking at it makes my heart hurt. It makes me want to hold him and protect him from any other pain he might have to suffer through.

"That's the one," I say to myself. "That's a face that could change minds."

I draw what I see, not just Bugsy's face but the way he makes me feel. I draw his heart and his sorrow. I draw his survival too. Everything feels so right, until Duffy's face pops up. Then poof! The moment is shattered.

"You'll never guess," Duffy whispers with sheer urgency. "Those servers Silver Tips talked about?"

"Her name is Miss S.," I remind him.

"Whatever," he says. "The servers, the WoW servers, they're working now. In fact, they're probably working all the time. And guess who has the password!" He waves a scrap of bright yellow paper in the air.

"Shut up!" I say. "Let me see it." I pull up my WoW launch page, enter my username and the password Duffy supplied and—voilà! Hippocrates appears before my eyes.

"Sweet!" Duffy says.

"Dangerous," I say. But I have no idea how true that is until Pompom appears on my friend list.

"Hi, Hippo," she says. "Got a minute for a quick dungeon? My tank character's about your level, and you can be the healer. Queue time should be super short."

Amazing! This high-level goddess wants me to be the healer in her party. How can I say no? Besides, I've made a strong start on my art project and Duffy is here to queue up too.

So that's three out of five of the players we need even before we start.

"Sounds great," I type. "Can my friend Duffy, I mean, Cyrano join our party?"

"Tell him to saddle up," she says. Duffy runs to the PC like it's Christmas morning.

"Let's do this thing," I say. And the chaos begins.

With Pompom and I queued up as the tank and healer, our wait time evaporates. Duffy and two strangers step up to deal damage, and we're in. But a part of me is terrified. It's great to feel needed as THE healer. But if I let Pompom down, I may never heal again.

"It's going to take everything I've got," I say out loud before I swallow hard and dive in.

Pompom looks so cute as a pandaren tank, her black and purple hair crowned with a burst of flowers. Duffy thinks so too.

"Hey, teddy bear, remember me?" he types. His elf blows her a kiss. Heat rushes to my cheeks. Duffy's my best friend, but for a second I hate Cyrano.

"Oh yeah," Pompom types. "The rodeo clown. Did you ever learn how to dodge acid?"

I can hear Duffy's stifled chuckle, and I relax a little.

"Sure did," he types. "I can even lace my boots with help from Hippo."

"Good to hear," Pompom types. "This dungeon's full of dudes that spit acid. And make sure you let me draw in the goblins. They don't have much health to drain, but they really hit hard."

After schooling Duffy, Pompom turns to me. Her pandaren tank actually smiles. Yeah, she likes me. "Watch my back, okay, Hippo?" she says. I don't type it, but watching her has become one of my favorite hobbies.

"Always," is what I do type. "You can count on me." Then I hope (how I hope!) it's actually true.

"Great," she says. "This dungeon is beautiful, but it can take forever."

My heart skips a beat. "How long?" I type.

"A little longer than some," she says, "but I'll get us through it."

Like an electronic conscience, my phone vibrates in my pocket. If I leave now, I'll be on time for Miss Grayson's mandate. But if I leave now, Pompom has no healer. So I turn the alarm off, thinking just a couple more minutes. I'll say I got held up in the bathroom. No one wants to talk about passing a deuce.

Pompom leads us through an underwater metropolis, and it's magnificent. It's overgrown with corals and crawling with starfish. Magic keeps us dry, but it's as if we are a part of the watery landscape. Sea life darts across our path, and it's distracting, but I focus on Pompom's back.

Every enemy encounter boosts my confidence. Her tank health falls, but my white light brings it back again. My magic bubble-like shield absorbs goblin blow after goblin blow. And magic spells heal Duffy and the other two warriors too. But the clock is ticking, and we're not even half done.

After vanquishing a monstrous behemoth with a tentacle face and arms like battle clubs, we come to the end of a long hallway and wait in a large, empty room.

"We have to wait for the elevator," Pompom says, collapsing on her character's knees. I move Hippocrates to sit right beside her.

"At least the view is nice," I type. I'm looking at Pompom, but the scene is mind-blowing too. We have a 360-degree view of the ocean surrounding us. The massive tentacles of what could be the dungeon's final boss wrap around the chamber, but we are out of reach. And sunlight dances through the water like liquefied crystal. I can tell the artists who created it slaved over every detail to transcend the ordinary—to deliver a masterpiece.

"This is my favorite dungeon," Pompom types. "I love the ocean."

I wish I could say I love it too. But I can love this place, here, with her. "I hope I can draw stuff like this someday," I say instead.

"You're an artist?!" I can almost hear her enthusiasm though the text. "Me too! Well, I want to be. I'm not that great."

I'm grinning like an idiot now. Of course she's an artist. She's perfect. "What kind of stuff do you draw?"

"I like designing characters and outfits," she says. "But backgrounds and stuff are boring. I want to be a concept artist for the game someday."

"That'd be so great," I type. "I bet you can do it."

The elevator finally arrives, and I'm almost sorry.

"Back to work," she types. "Ready?"

My laptop slams shut before I can answer.

"Game over," the night librarian says. "Your

school called, and you're fifty minutes late for your second-period class. Report to your principal's office, immediately."

How did the time pass so quickly? I wonder. Then another question swallows the first like a wounded guppy. How will I explain all of this to my dad?

CHAPTER SEVEN
Father Knows Best

Wednesday Night

Seeing the principal so disappointed is bad.
Seeing Miss Grayson upset is bone-crushing.
She is my favorite teacher, and she trusted
me to be responsible. I could see on her face
that I really let her down, but I have no idea
how to make it right. Dad held his temper in
the office as they explained my offenses—
ditching second period to play video games
online at the library. Oversimplified, to my

way of thinking, but I'm not about to argue.
Not today.

Two days' suspension. Case closed.

The car ride home is silent. Not a word.
Not a murmur. Not a sigh. When we get
home, Dad takes my laptop and heads for the
kitchen to drink some milk out of the carton.
His stomach must be bothering him, and milk
usually helps. I stand there, waiting for him to
chew me out, but the silence continues.

"I'm going to the basement," I say. Still, my
dad says nothing.

I shuffle down the stairs, rub Bugsy's head,
and sit down to play WoW on the old desktop
computer. The power cable is gone. My
phone's charger is gone too. A note says, "No
television, iPad, or iPod either." Suspension
isn't my only punishment. Part of me wants
the escape of WoW, but I don't know how long
this technology grounding is going to last and
maybe I should ration the remaining battery
on my phone. I decide to take Bugsy outside.

"We're going for a walk," I say to Dad, expecting the silence to hold.

"Ten minutes," he says. His tone says the time constraint is not up for debate.

Bugsy senses trouble but leaves it in the house as we exit. He is so happy to be on the prowl, happy to be prowling with me. He's probably the only one who likes me right now. A text pings my phone, and even without looking, I know it's Duffy.

"You okay?" he says. He knows my dad must be REALLY mad.

"Silent treatment," I respond. "You okay?"

"Totally," he says. "My mom was just relieved I wasn't dead."

Suddenly, I start to miss my mom. I don't remember much about her. I remember she was sunny and lively and fun. I remember she used to sing to me before I fell asleep at night and every morning as I woke up. Nursery rhymes, pop songs, commercial jingles—whatever she thought would make me smile. But I sure wasn't smiling when she left.

"I can't breathe here," she said, packing the biggest suitcase I'd ever seen. "Your dad never lets me breathe." She didn't promise to come back for me. She didn't apologize. She just walked away, as if I was never born. And suddenly, I was the one who couldn't breathe. Maybe I don't miss her after all.

"How mad was Pompom?" I ask.

"She was pretty ticked off, but I explained when I got home. She just thinks you're an outlaw now. I did you proud."

And I thought things couldn't get worse. Duffy has convinced the girl I like that I'm some kind of punk rebel. And I have no way of setting that right, either. Maybe Pompom is a real rebel since she was playing during school hours too.

"Are you grounded?" Duffy texts, as if he's read my mind. I text back a frowning emoji. "No WoW tournament, either?"

I text another frown. "I'll work on my history project tonight."

"Sounds like a plan," he texts. "But what about tomorrow and Friday?"

I don't even want to think about tomorrow, and my ten minutes are about to expire so I say, "Who knows?" and head for home.

"I'm back," I say, more to be sure he knows I'm on time than for a response. Nothing. "Going to go finish my history project." Nothing. I don't know what he's thinking. But I like it better when he's mad out loud.

With Bugsy as a life model, I finish the poster I started at the library in the next couple of hours. I hand letter the final slogan across the top of the page. FIGHT THE LIES, NOT THE DOGS. At the bottom, in script I write, PIT BULLS ARE BORN TO LOVE. I sign it, Austin. Just Austin.

"I'm going to bed now," I yell to my dad.

"Set your alarm for five o'clock," he says. "You're going to work with me."

On a normal day, I would have argued. Today, I didn't dare.

CHAPTER EIGHT
A Whale of a Tale

Thursday

Waking up at five o'clock shouldn't be so hard, but today it's like raising the dead. I picture Hippocrates slipping on swim trunks and a T-shirt to shadow my dad.

"Weather report calls for clear skies today, so put on plenty of sunscreen," he hollers. "Your skin isn't used to the light."

He's hurled a stereotypical slam against gamers, and it's not even five thirty. But in this case, he happens to be right. I haven't hung out on the bay since my mom left. So I slather it on thick and reach for my cell phone.

"No cell phone," he says, grabbing his backpack. "It's a no-technology kind of day, and it's time to go." My stomach rumbles, and we both hear it. I haven't had breakfast, but it doesn't faze him. "We'll grab something on the way," he says. "You can throw it back when we get on the boat."

"Which boat?" I ask, hoping it's the Sea Chaser. That little speedboat is a blast on a warm, sunny day. But I'll be thankful for anything—and I do mean anything—other than the two-man dinghy. Rowing that thing across the bay is torture.

"Not the Chaser," he says as we climb into his truck. "Not today. What do you want to eat?"

We drive through Mickey D's, and I order an egg sandwich and an orange juice.

"Better make it two," Dad says. "You're going to need the fuel."

Oh, God, I think doing a facepalm. *We're going to take the dinghy. I better make it three.*

I follow Dad into the office, and all of his coworkers say hello.

"Pudge, my man," his assistant Cody says, smiling. "I can't believe you've gotten so big. What are you now, sixteen?"

"Fourteen," I answer. "Only two more years and I can drive."

"Not if you don't clean up your act," Dad says.

"Ahhh," Cody says laughing. "What did you do to tick off the old man?"

"He ditched a class to play video games at the library," Dad says, shuffling through a dozen clipboards. But for some reason, he doesn't seem mad.

"Way to go, gamer dude," Cody says. "Let me guess. There was a girl involved, am I right?"

"Where there's trouble," Dad says, "there's a girl." And I wonder, how did he know?

"You'll learn a thing or two today," he continues. "And I won't even have to pay tuition."

"Dinghy duty?" Cody asks, and Dad nods. "Oh, man," Cody continues. "After you learn whatever your dad is teaching, take it from me. Learn the fine art of not getting caught."

Dad shoots him a look, but I can tell he's trying not to smile. Who is this guy? And what has he done with my dad? I'm about to find out.

"To the dinghy," Dad says tossing me a pair of leather work gloves. "There are whales to survey and not a minute to lose." We hike down the pier, and he nods toward the center's new rowboat. "Climb in," he says, tossing his backpack and a clipboard in.

It isn't easy for a big kid to board a tiny boat without a whole lot of rocking. I'm afraid I'm about to take a swim, but the boat settles, and I sit down to eat and wait for my dad. He unties the moorings and pushes the boat away from the dock. Like a dancer, he swivels and glides his body into the boat. He's really graceful and so clearly in his element.

"Grab the oars and head northwest," he says. "I want to try to check a few of the whale tags. In the dinghy, we'll get as close as we can." Huh, I think. It's not just punishment.

Once I hit a rhythm, the rowing isn't so bad. I like the sound of the oars slicing into the water and the smell of fish and salt floating in the air. Seagulls circle above, wondering if we have minnows to share. And sea lions watch us from rocky perches rising up out of the Pacific. I can see why Pompom loves this. And I have to admit, Dad probably feels the same.

"Stop," he whispers as he grabs a pair of field glasses. "Do you see it? It's a new calf, a baby. It probably isn't even tagged. But where is its mother? Can you see it, Pudge? Look closely. It's right over there."

I lean forward, trying to look where my father is pointing, but it's too far away. I can't see a thing. So he hands me the binoculars and guides my head to the perfect angle. And there it is—a baby humpback whale, fluttering through the San Francisco Bay.

"Holy cow, Dad," I say. I am practically speechless. All I can think is how big he is and, at the same time, how incredibly small. I put the field glasses down just long enough to watch my father. There are tears in his eyes and running down his cheek as he whispers to the baby. But I can't make out what he's trying to say.

I search for the baby again in the binoculars and almost immediately find him. But he's swimming next to what looks like a pile of floating trash. "Dad," I say, "is it safe for the baby to play with that garbage?"

He takes the glasses from me and lets out an audible gasp as a stream of water shoots up from the heap of seaweed and plastic and rope. "That's not fishing debris, Pudge. That's the baby's mom. And if we don't hurry, neither one of them will survive."

I've read about this. They call it ghost fishing. Nets tangled in the sea aren't always retrieved. Fishermen cut them lose and sail away. Maybe they think it doesn't matter, but it does. Because sea creatures still get trapped and without anyone to free them, they grow exhausted and eventually drown. It's a really big problem.

"Not today, Dad," I say. He falls backwards as the boat jolts into motion. I row hard toward the tangled mother. I row hard because there is something so important for us to do. For the first time in years, my dad and I are on the same team.

As we approach the adult whale, she shows clear signs of panic, so we have to work quickly. Dad reaches into his backpack to retrieve his knife. "I don't want you to worry," he says, "but I'm going to have to cut her free."

"You're jumping into the water with a fifty-foot carnivore defending her calf?" I say. "Are you crazy?"

"Probably," he says. "But remember, she's a carnivore that eats tiny little shrimp, not people. And some risks—well, this risk is worth taking."

I know he's right, so I nod. "What should I do?"

"Try to distract the baby," he says as he removes his shirt and shoes. He holds the knife in his left hand and steadies himself with the right. Just as he's poised to jump into the water feetfirst something slams into the dinghy— something big. Dad is sent flying and lands horizontal—back first—against the boat seat with a slam. The knife jams deep into the flesh of his right arm, and he cries out.

"Ouch!" he screams. "Isn't this just great! Just what we really needed." A trickle of blood drips around the quivering knife now protruding from his arm as he pulls himself up and takes a seat in the dinghy.

"Ouch?" I ask. "You've been impaled on a giant dagger, and all you can say is ouch?"

"What?" he says, embarrassed. "I was never very good at swearing."

I shake my head. Then the reality hits me. My father has been stabbed, and this is not a video game. He doesn't seem worried as he turns to study the wound, but I'm worried enough for both of us. "How can I help?" I say. "Should I pull it out? Of course not, you'll bleed to death if I pull it out. You're going to have to help me here. What do you want me to do?"

"Watch less television?" he asks. I shake my head. "Okay," he says. "Take a deep breath. Then ask yourself, do you see a lot of blood? Do you really think it hit a vein?"

I focus and realize my dad is a genius. "It only hit muscle," I say. "Probably hurts like crazy, but you're not going to die."

"Not today," he says. And in spite of the pain, my father smiles.

"Pull it out," he says. "We'll use my shirt as a temporary bandage until we can head back to the office. What hit us, anyway? Did you see?"

"I think it was the baby," I say as I use his knife to cut his shirt to ribbons—sloppy strips of cloth I hope will stop the bleeding, but I'm a kid. Seriously, what do I know about healing real flesh and blood? "Was he trying to defend his mother?"

"Nah," Dad says. "He was probably just trying to play. But we have a new problem." I finish wrapping his arm and listen. "The mother whale is still in danger. If we don't cut her free, she will die. And without her, Junior will die too."

"The knife hit your right arm," I say. He nods. "And you're right-handed." He nods. "So it has to be me."

"I know you don't like to swim," he says, "but you've had all the lessons. Technically, you know what to do, and it's a pretty calm day. Are you up for the challenge? I'm behind you if you say no. We can't save every whale, and I want you to feel safe."

He looks deep into my eyes, thinking I'll

bow out. But I can't let that happen. "I'm in," I say. "We're not going to make that baby an orphan."

I've made up my mind. So he leans out over the far side of the dinghy. That way I can slip into the water on the other side without capsizing the dinghy. Once I'm safely treading water, he hands me the knife.

"Work quickly," he says. "She hasn't got much time."

I'm only a few feet from the enormous marine mammal, and she's too bound up to defend herself, but I can't help feeling awestruck by the sheer size and physical power wrapped in fishing trash. Such a noble creature shouldn't face death in such a senseless fashion. She deserves better, I think.

Slowly, I swim toward her, whispering reassurances. I know she doesn't speak my language, but I hope she'll understand my tone. "You're a beauty," I say, "and I only want to help." She sends air and water hissing through her blowhole, and I wonder if she's trying to talk to me too.

In seconds, I am at her side. I run my hand across the smooth, dark flesh of the whale's massive head and gaze into her dark brown eye. "No lashes," I think, but I do see determination. She wants to win this fight, and I want to make sure she does.

My leg muscles are already burning, so I talk more to distract myself from the pain.

"Do you have a name?" I ask, making my way to her first pectoral fin. Every inch of her is covered in rope and twine and plastic, so I cut and carve as I go.

"Can I call you Pompom?" I ask. "I know a girl called Pompom. She's a lot like you. She can take a ton of damage and still walk away. Not me, though. I can't take a punch, but I can sure help heal one. So my job is to keep watch over her. If she's hit too hard, I can ease the pain. I hope that's what I'm doing for you."

The tangle of garbage has grown so tight that it's cutting into her skin. I can see the raw flesh, even under the water. It has to really hurt, but she doesn't flinch when I touch her. In fact, she doesn't resist me at all. It's like she knows I'm here to help.

"Good girl," I whisper as I cut more net. And just so it will never hurt another marine animal again, I toss every scrap into the bottom of the boat. Dad is a master at paddling that dinghy, even with one arm. He hovers next to us without once hitting me or the whale.

"Be careful of the fluke," Dad says as I approach her tail. "She can use that as a weapon if she feels threatened." I agree, but I know she won't hurt me. We're in this together now. I cut her tail free, running my fingers across scars that look like they've been there for decades.

"See those marks?" he asks. "That's how we tell the whales apart. No two scar patterns are the same. To us, they're like fingerprints."

"So she's been carved up too," I say. "You have that in common."

He laughs.

Suddenly, every part of my body is aching. I'm seriously struggling as I come full circle and cut the last piece from her face. It slips out of my hand and starts to sink, but the baby appears out of nowhere and bumps it back into my hands. I glance at my father, totally amazed.

"They like to play," he reminds me as I toss the rescued piece into the boat. Then his face turns serious. "You've done really well, Pudge. She'll be okay now," he says. "I think we better call it a day. Climb into the boat, and we'll head back to shore."

I take one last look at this magnificent creature, and I feel the need to thank her. "You've given me so much," I say. "How will I ever repay you?"

"You saved her life," Dad says. "And the life of her baby. I'd say the debt is paid."

"Fair enough," I say as I hand him the knife. I grip the side with both hands and try to lift myself over, but it's not happening. It was a lot easier to get out of the boat than it is to get back in. It's as if my muscles are failing me. I should have paid more attention in PE.

I take a deep breath and try it again. But again, it's a miserable fail. "I don't think I have the energy," I say. So Dad holds out his good arm to help me. I try to grip his hand, but I can't hold on, and neither can he. I simply weigh too much to lift. My fear factor is definitely rising.

"Try again," Dad barks. But I can't find the strength to climb at all.

"Listen, Austin," he says. "I don't want to scare you, but it's go time. We're on the verge of do or die. Do you understand me?"

I'm suddenly so tired, I can barely focus, but I know he called my name. "You said Austin," I say. "I love it when you say my name. But I'm going to take a little nap now. We'll talk after I've had a chance to rest." I fall back and float like an ocean angel.

"No," he screams. "Don't go to sleep. Don't give up on us now."

His voice fades, and I find myself in that game dungeon with Pompom. She's sitting next to me, and we're holding hands. I am totally at peace.

"Are we floating?" I ask her.

"Yes, we are," she says. "Just lie back and I'll carry you home."

I don't hear Dad cursing the man who took the life jackets and the walkie-talkie out of the dinghy. I don't know he's trying to reach me with the wooden oar or saying he can't bear to lose me and my mother too. All I can hear is Pompom humming as I slip into a deeper sleep.

"Is this how I die?" I ask her. "Trying to save a mother whale?"

"Is that what you were doing?" she asks. "Cool. That's as good a way as any. Better than most."

"Yeah," I say. "At least I didn't choke on a pretzel."

She laughs and says, "You didn't pull an Elvis and die on the toilet."

"I didn't get my face torn off by a chimpanzee."

"True," she says with a snort. "Hey, maybe you didn't die at all."

BAM!

Something strikes and jolts me out of my dream—something big and powerful and unyielding. The pointed nose of a whale hits the small of my back, and the sting takes my breath away. I choke on the water that's splashed into my mouth. All the while, she rises out of the brine, and I rise with her. Then, in an instant, the upward motion reverses, and I am literally airborne.

I am falling, and I think it's to my death. But I land in the belly of a dinghy where my father is crying like a baby. "Thank you," he says looking out on the horizon. I rise up on my elbows just long enough to see the humpback's fluke splash against the water, as if she's waving good-bye. Then the world goes black.

When I come to, we are halfway to the marina. The bandages I made are now soaked in crimson, and my dad is in pretty bad shape. "Move," I say as I prepare to row us home. Dad pulls a water bottle from his backpack, and we drain it in seconds flat.

"They'll never believe it," he says.

"That's okay," I answer. "I'm not sure I believe it myself."

When I finally step out onto the old wooden pier, I feel like I could cry. It's been such a horrible, wonderful day that I don't know how to make sense of it. And there is my dad, tearing up beside me. He drapes his good arm around my shoulders as we walk past the office and straight to the truck.

"Am I still grounded?" I ask as he hands me the key to put into the ignition. Some guys couldn't drive with one arm sliced and bleeding. But my dad isn't one of those guys. He just finds a way to get it done.

"I don't know," he whispers. "Ask me after they stitch up my arm."

We buckle up, and I help him put the truck in drive. I lean my head against the window and almost instantly fall asleep. At this moment, it doesn't matter what he decides.

CHAPTER NINE
First-Class Propaganda

Friday

Dad is sitting at the kitchen table when I wake up the next morning at eleven o'clock. Fifteen stitches and a sling win him the day off, and I'm still officially suspended. Every inch of my body is on fire, so believe it or not, I'm glad.

"Hey, Austin," he says. "Did you sleep okay?"

"I did if you count dreams of swimming with marine animals all night going to sleep."

"Welcome to my world," he says with a smile. And for once I know he means it.

I sit down and feel tears welling up in my eyes. "Dad," I say, "I just want you to know, I'm really sorry I disappointed you and Miss Grayson."

"I know you are," he says. "Did you get the assignment finished Wednesday?"

"Yeah," I answer. "But I got most of it done at the library. I can't draw when people are watching. That's why I asked to do it off campus. And that's what I did until Duffy got the Internet password and we lost track of time."

"It doesn't sound like you meant to screw up."

"I didn't," I say, "but I really messed up with Miss Grayson."

"Give it some time," he says. "She'll remember who you really are. Can I see the finished project?"

I hand him the final poster, and it's his turn to get sentimental. "Austin," he says. "I had no idea you were so talented. I thought you were still drawing skateboards and pirate skulls, but this is truly exceptional. Isn't it due today? Let's take it to Miss Grayson and see what she thinks of your skills."

We drive to the school and look for Miss Grayson. "There she is," I tell him, pointing to the pretty dark-haired teacher with cat-eye glasses.

"Cute," he says.

"What?" I say. "Did my father just hit on my history teacher?"

"Not yet," he says, "but give me a little time."

He shoots me a cheesy smile over his shoulder that reminds me of Duffy, then makes his way to Miss Grayson. The guy I saw crying in a rowboat is transformed into the aquatic god I've always envied, and my teacher is loving it. She listens, rapt, to whatever it is he's saying. She bites her lip, touches her face, and then his arm in the sling. Finally, she softly laughs as he leans in to whisper. Their eyes turn to me.

"Austin," he says, waving me over with his good arm. Miss Grayson leans toward him and affectionately smiles.

"Your dad's explained everything to me," she says, "so let's just put this behind us and move forward to the good days coming next."

"I'd like that," I say. "And I finished my assignment." I hand her the foam-mounted artwork, and she lifts the tissue paper cover sheet. Her hand flies up to her mouth as she takes it in, the presentation, the drawing, the slogan, and the way it mirrors the propaganda book that she loaned me.

"It's beautiful," she says softly, "so much more than I expected. But do you have your bibliography? I hate to ask."

"Here it is," I say, handing her the second half of the finished work. "I really did take this seriously."

"I can see you did," she says. "Please know

I really appreciate it. You've raised a remarkable young man," she says to my dad. "I hope you know it."

"I haven't always given him his due," he admits. "But I'm determined to make that right."

"That's half the battle," she says. "Love will take you a long, long way."

"Thank you, Miss Grayson," I say. "See you Monday morning."

"Bright and sunny," she says. I never noticed before how much she was like my dad.

As we walk back to the truck, my dad nudges me with his shoulder. "She is cute," he says, "and smart. And she's right, love can take us a long way."

I smile.

"You know I do, right?" he asks.

"Do what," I say. I know what he means, but I'm going to make him say it.

"Love you," he says. "You know I do, right?"

"Yeah, I guess I do," I say. "And I love you too, Dad."

"Good. Now that we've got that settled," he says, "I have to ask you another question. Who the heck is Pompom?"

I laugh. "As soon as I get my power cable back, I'll show you," I say.

"I have a better idea," he says, "why don't you show me at the library's WoW tournament tonight, assuming I can tag along."

"Sure thing," I say. And I am amazed.

For the first time in a long time, my dad and I totally agree.

Austin's story is fiction, but animal conservationists sometimes have the chance to save whales from the garbage humans create. On December 11, 2005, commercial fisherman and whale-watching tour guide Mick Menigoz contacted six professional divers from the Marine Mammal Center in Sausalito, California. A fifty-foot, fifty-ton female humpback was tangled in discarded crab traps, nets, and fishing lines about eighteen miles from the coast of San Francisco. Without help, she would almost certainly tire and drown.

According to the *San Francisco Chronicle*, the divers worked for hours using special curved knives to cut the dangerous garbage from the whale's body. Forty-year-old James Moskito was the first one in the water.

"My heart sank when I saw all the lines wrapped around it," he said in the *Chronicle*. "I really didn't think we were going to be able to save it." But save her they did. The gentle giant hovered quietly as the men fought to give her a second chance. When they had finished, the whale allegedly moved from diver to diver to give them each a gentle nudge.

"It seemed kind of affectionate, like a dog that's happy to see you," Moskito said in the newspaper. "I never felt threatened. It was an amazing, unbelievable experience."

Before the year 1900, approximately fifteen thousand humpbacks thrived in the North Pacific. Thousands were lost to commercial fishing, but their protected status may save them from extinction, assuming that protected status holds.

ABOUT THE AUTHOR

Kelly Milner Halls went whale watching in Ventura, California, as a kid, but she never saw a single fluke. In fact, she got seasick and saw the bottom of a garbage can most of the day. But she hasn't given up and hopes to experience the magic one of these days.

Until then, she donates to several whale-friendly charities and hopes the day will come when fishing for whales is only a shameful memory of the past and all whales navigate the oceans with joy and no fear. She also hopes to write a nonfiction book on ghost fishing.

She lives in Spokane, Washington, with two daughters, two dogs, too many cats, and a five-foot rock iguana named Gigantor. Her low-level blood elf priest is just aching to meet Pompom and Hippo and run a few dungeons of her own. Read more about Kelly and her books at www.wondersofweird.com. E-mail her at kellymilnerh@aol.com.

Check out all the books in
the ANIMAL RESCUES series:

ANIMAL RESCUES
#1
blazing courage

KELLY MILNER HALLS

ANIMAL RESCUES
#2
dive into danger

KELLY MILNER HALLS